Grandma, What is Cancer?

Written and Illustrated by Mary Jo Prado

Copyright© 2008 MJ Daley-Prado
First Publication 2008

Second Publication 2014
Copyright©2014

Printed By: Createspace
United States of America

ISBN-13: 978-1499720433
ISBN-10: 1499720432

Dedications

This book dedicated in the memory of:

My mother, Shirley A. Daley
and my sister, Shirley A. Danlag

To two of the most courageous woman I know. They fought valiantly but sadly, both lost their battles to cancer. May their eternal flame burn bright and light the path so that others may heal.

To my dad, Leonard, a breast cancer survivor.

Acknowledgements

To Francessca
Thank you for being so patient.
I love you.

To Satish
Thank you for giving this project wings.
I am lucky to be able to call you my best friend as you
are one in every sense of the word.

"Grammy, Miss Sandy said Mommy has cancer," Susie's voice quivered.

Something wasn't right.

She didn't understand why everyone kept talking in hushed tones. "Grandma, what is cancer?" asked Susie.

"Ah, sweetheart, **cancer** is a disease that women and some men get. Your mommy felt a tiny lump right here." Her grandma pointed to her own chest.

"The doctor did a special test called a **mammogram**. The mammogram showed the doctor Mommy has a disease called breast cancer. It's sort of like when you fall and get a boo-boo. Well, some people with cancer have boo-boos inside their bodies. You see Susie, there are all kinds of cancers."

"How will the doctors fix my mommy, Grandma?" Susie asked.

"The doctors will give Mommy a very strong medicine called **chemotherapy**. Mommy will go to the hospital or a special clinic for a few days."

"Doctors will give the chemotherapy through a special needle and tube that will be placed in her arm. This needle is called an **IV**. Some people have a special needle called a **port**. This is placed into a person's neck or chest. The doctors may need to give Mommy **radiation.** Do you remember your X-ray?" asked Grandma.

Susie nodded.

"Well, the doctors can use those machines to help Mommy. It's a procedure called radiation. These procedures will make Mommy very sick and weak, sweetie. Mommy won't feel like doing anything for quite some time," Grandma said.

Susie sat quietly for a few minutes thinking about everything her grandma had said. "Is she going to puke?" Susie needed to know.

Grandma couldn't help but chuckle. "Mommy is going to get an upset stomach and she will probably feel like throwing up. We will have to help her do many things, like wash dishes, help make dinner. You can help by picking up your toys."

"Will Mommy get skinny?"

"She may, honey. It depends on how she handles the chemotherapy."

"What else will happen?" Susie asked.

"Mommy may lose her hair," Grandma said.

"Do you mean she's going to look like my Poppie?" Susie giggled.

"Oh, you silly goose." Grandma tickled Susie's belly. "No, she's not going to look like your Poppie! Your Mommy is much prettier."

"Oh, Grandma!"

"Well, she is!" Grandma smiled.

"Can we buy Mommy a pretty hat, Grandma? Can we try to find one with pretty flowers on it...please pretty please? Can we, Grandma? Can we?"

Grandma nodded. "Sure of course we can, honey. I think Mommy will like that very much. Susie, things are going to be a little different and a bit difficult but we will get through this together."

"Will Mommy need a wheelchair, Grandma?

"We may need to push Mommy in a **wheelchair**."

"Why?" asked Susie.

"Well, there will be days when Mommy will feel too sick or weak to stand and she's going to need extra help."

"Can I ride too?" She looked up at her grandma with pleading eyes.

"Maybe, if you're good. We will have to see what Mommy says."

"What else, Grandma?"

"Mommy might get a little grumpy. If Mommy asks you to do something please listen okay, Susie? I don't want your mommy to have to ask you over and over. Whatever Mommy asks of you please do as she says and make things easier okay, sweetheart?"

"I will Grandma," said Susie. "Pinkie promise."

"Honey, Mommy might get quite sick and weak from the chemotherapy but you don't need to feel afraid though because Grandma and Poppie will be here with you. We will take great care of both you and Mommy." Grandma kissed Susie on her forehead. "What's wrong, pumpkin? Why the long face?"

"Grandma, is my mommy going to die? Will she? Tommy's Uncle had cancer and he died." Susie looked down. "Tommy said my mommy is going to die too."

"Oh, Susie, sweetie. No one really knows what will happen. Right now, we have to think good thoughts. We have to pray every day that God will bless your Mommy and help the doctors make Mommy well again."

Susie cracked a smile.

"Try not to worry dear and if you have any questions please come to me or your daddy and we will do our best to answer them for you." Grandma kissed Susie on her forehead and gave her a big super-duper bear hug.

"Grandma—" Susie inhaled a deep breath. "I can't breathe."

"Oops. I'm sorry, sweetie." Grandma smiled.

"I love you, Grandma. I'm glad you're here."

"I love you too, sweetheart and so does your mommy."

A Note from the Author:

Cancer is one of the leading causes of death in the United States today. Research continues every day and there have been medical advances. The one area that lacks that same response is helping our young children cope with the illness and possibly a death of a loved one.

My sister was diagnosed with breast cancer at the tender age of thirty-three. Shirley was Mom to four young children all between the ages of five and twelve. My sister was compassionately cared for by Hospice and her family. We wanted my sister to be surrounded by unlimited love so we each took turns caring for her. After a six-year long battle, my sister lost her life to breast cancer in August 1998.

During this difficult time, we searched for inspirational books for our children and came up empty-handed. Many of the books we found were filled with doom and gloom. There were no books for young children at that time.

I attempted to write *Grandma, What is Cancer?* many times but grief got in the way. When my mother died in 2003, she made me promise that I would write this book. So, with that said, I hope this book has helped you and your family in some small way.

May God Bless You and Heal your family.

MJ Daley-Prado

Websites that offer emotional, spiritual, and financial support

The National Children's Cancer Society
www.thenccs.org

American Cancer Society
www.cancer.org/treatment/childrenandcancer

Friends of Kids with Cancer
www.friendsofkids.com

I'm Too Young for this
www.usoncology.com/network/Misc/Websites?p_url=ww
w.imtooyoungforthis.org

Chemo Angels
www.chemoangels.wix.com/chemo-angels-1/

Breast Cancer
www.breastcancer.org/community

Breast Cancer Support
www.bcsupport.org/

Susan G. Komen
ww5.komen.org/BreastCancer/SupportGroups.html

Caring Bridge
www.caringbridge.org/

My Life Line
www.mylifeline.org/

A place to write your feelings....

_____

_____

_____

_____

_____

_____

_____

Special Photographs

Special Photographs

CPSIA information can be obtained
at www.ICGtesting.com
Printed in the USA
LVHW071925120423
744162LV00002B/69

9 781499 720433